Ah remember hearin' that. Twasn't a storm Ah heard, but some beastie?

"After a fashion."

A bright flash of lightning lit the sky the same moment an explosion of sound washed over the ship. Suddenly the vessel pitched on the wind. Crewmen clung to nearby hand holds, belaying pins, rigging, whatever stable surface they could find. Before the ship settled, it lurched once more. A hard groan of timbers followed a pair of sharp pops. Krumer and O'Fallon exchanged a glance.

"Ah'd be knowin' pistol shot e'en in this storm. Near the bow Ah be thinkin'."

"Where the Captain is!"

Hunter's voice cut through the howl of wind, "All hands! To arms!"

Tales of the Brass Griffin: Red Lightning

C. B. Ash

Red Lightning

Other fine books by C. B. Ash:

Kinloch Novels:

Kinloch

Tales of the Brass Griffin Novels:

Red Lightning
Children's Tale
Dead Air
Bloody Business
Dead Men's Tales
The Seventh Knife*

*Currently viewable on http://brassgriffin.com

This book is a work of fiction. All the characters, events and locations portrayed in this book are either fictitious or are used fictionally. Any resemblance to actual persons, living or dead, events, or locales is entirely coincidental.

TALES OF THE BRASS GRIFFIN: RED LIGHTNING

Copyright © 2013 by Christopher B Ash

ISBN: 978-0-578-02356-4

First Edition: May 2009
Second Edition: Jan 2012
Third Edition: Sept 2013

For everyone who looked up in the sky and dreamed … "what if"

Please … Keep on dreaming.

Chapter 1

Winds howled and rain hammered at the sails, like the sharp rapping of a drum. Clouds boiled and twisted, as if stirred by an unseen hand. Amid this maelstrom, lightning arced across the clouds, turning night to day in the oppressive gloom.

Deep among the gray, churning clouds, the airship's cabin shook from the roar of thunder. Outside, high winds beat mercilessly against the *Brass Griffin*'s worn wooden and copper hull. Wet rigging popped as it slapped against one another, and against the tight, wet canvas of the airship's elongated gas bag that kept it aloft.

With a heavy groan, the cabin door protested at being pulled open from outside. A tall, olive-skinned figure appeared in the doorway. Standing a good two inches past six feet, he wore a loose blue shirt, brown cotton trousers and dripping wet rain slicker. Long black hair drawn back into a rough collection of braids framed a stern face. He wiped rainwater from his eyes with the back of a sleeve.

"Captain! We've reached the storm's heart," the broad-shouldered man said.

Across the room, Captain Anthony Hunter memorized the page number in front of him, closing the old, leather bound volume of "King Solomon's Mines" and setting it on a small table beside him.

The captain was a tall, square-built man with thick shoulders in a plain white cotton shirt. He tugged at the old leather vest he wore, the one dotted with the occasional bullet scars, to straighten it. As he did so, he reached into a vest pocket instinctively, remembering at the last moment that his pocket watch was no longer there. With a sigh, he quickly combed a hand through his brown hair, cut short in the Royal Navy style, that was touched with a hint of gray at the temples.

"Very good, Mr. Whitehorse. What sign?"

Winds thrust at the ship again, threatening to turn the vessel broadsides. "Hail in the lower clouds, lightning here on high," the olive-skinned crewman replied.

Hunter nodded, then stood, strapping on a pair of brass-trimmed wheel-lock pistols before throwing on a worn long coat for protection against the elements.

"Good. Lightning nets deployed?"

"Right before we crested the cloud bank."

"Well done. Once we've refueled, we can light the furnace and process some of that ore we picked up at Chapman's mining camp." He paused to listen to the rage of weather outside. "Quite the storm. If we can spare a barrel-cell or two, we could sell it on market. It'd make some blacksmith or engineer very happy."

"Aye sir, true enough." Krumer started to move back on deck, but paused when he noticed Hunter was not behind him. "Captain?"

Hunter flexed his artificial left hand, gears and clockwork mechanisms opening and closing his brass and leather fingers obediently. "Just the hand again, Krumer. Ghost aches and pains."

"Bad omen, that. Last time it ached, a vampire had stowed away," Whitehorse shrugged.

"I still doubt the two were related. Besides, you're only

irritated because he locked you below decks," Hunter replied.

The first mate made a sour face, "he tied me like a game bird and stuffed me in the ship's stores! I still owe him for that insult."

Captain Hunter ignored the phantom ache in his artificial hand and reached for a glove to tug over it.

"Fortunately, he didn't make a light meal out of your tough orcish Canadian hide. I understand your feelings, however I'd like to lay hands upon him myself. He stole my best pocket watch, not to mention a week's worth of supplies and our best steam glider before setting out for whatever port he finally landed on. Speaking of which, how far out from a port are we?"

"Mr. Baker says no more than three days' strong sail for Briggs' Reach. Five for London proper. Not much here, this far north over the Ardennes."

"Not surprising. We're off the main route a bit."

Suddenly the ship lurched violently, knocking both men off their feet. Hunter glanced around, grasping for a handhold. The room itself was a common room that joined together the officer cabins aboard the *Griffin*. It was a box-like, with cabinets lining the walls. A long meeting table usually dominated the middle of the floor, but had been tossed to one side against a wall.

Maps and charts, normally stuffed away, were now tossed about the room. Cabinet doors stood open, their contents spilled out upon the floor. An empty bottle rolled past the captain's boot, unnoticed.

The captain's eyes searched the air, as if he could look into the seasoned wood and copper sheets of the ship itself for any damage. Krumer, accustomed to the captain's odd behaviors, had always accused Hunter of having the sense of a mystic when it came to ships. Anthony often ignored the remark, passing the comments down to good-natured ribbing. He simply knew his ship.

"That's more than just a gale of wind."

Scrambling to their feet, they raced to the deck.

Chapter 2

Outside, wind-swept rain beat on ship and crew alike. Clouds swirled like gray-black cream twisted about in a churn, tossing lighting like a child tosses a ball. Rain washed over the vessel in sheets, soaking anything in its path. In between the bursts of rain, wind howled like a thing, alive and angry.

The weathered canvas gas bag strained against the mooring ropes above, while the crew scrambled across the *Brass Griffin*'s deck. A trio of sailors struggled to stow the steering sails, fighting against the storm which greedily sought to steal the sailcloth, ropes and all. Others aboard pulled to secure an extra run of lines, specifically placed to help reinforce the airship's main gas bag to its collection of stout, hardwood masts.

As the door to the officer's cabins below the quarterdeck opened, a bright blast of lightning lashed out through the storm. The bolt of electricity engulfed one of the wire mesh nets that were extended out like metal gossamer wings on either side of the *Griffin's* hull. Coursing over the thin metal, it raced outward until it found the steel mooring lines and metal cables leading to the ship. The net and lines glowed, but instead of continuing the lightning - as the net was intended to do - the lines snapped with an ear-splitting shriek!

Krumer Whitehorse raced onto deck from the cabins beneath

the quarterdeck first, followed by Captain Hunter, close on his heels. The captain shielded his eyes against the rain, squinting as he searched for the source of the sound, while the first mate grabbed a gangly, brown-haired young man by the arm when he ran by.

"William, what happened?" Krumer asked leaning forward so the young man could hear.

William Falke pointed frantically at the starboard side of the bow. "Big bolt 'o red lightnin', mean as can be, arced over the starboard net. Burnt out the net's bow cables. Burnt 'em clear through."

"Anyone hurt?" Captain Hunter shouted over the storm.

"Nary a scratch, Cap'n," William replied.

"What of those stray lines?" Krumer asked quickly. "Has anyone tried to hook them back in reach?"

"Crew's tryin' ta secure the netting now to keep it from flailin' about anymore," William explained pointing towards a trio of his crew mates that were desperately trying to secure the metal net despite the loose cables whipping about. "We figure if we can just lash it down, it'll hold long enough ta make it through the storm."

"Belay that! Those cables could whip a hole through the ship's gas bag and cut any of us right in half in this storm. Just stow the starboard netting," the captain ordered, "as the net is pulled in, the cables will come with it. We'll make do with the port side."

"Cap'n, the batteries is plenty low," William replied.

"Rather short a few batteries than lose the ship or crew. If I have to, I'll get out and push! Now move! Let's get that net stowed!" Hunter growled at the crewman.

"Aye, Cap'n!" William replied sharply. "I'll pass the word!"

As William fought his way across the deck against the swirling wind, Mr. Whitehorse and Captain Hunter crossed the deck in another direction towards the main mast where Hunter could get a better view of the damage, while the crew at the bow worked at the rigging attached to the net. Ahead of the first mate and the captain, three crewmen worked feverishly at the lines to pull them under control.

Through the rain and storm, Anthony and Krumer could see the damage: blackened metal mesh, fluttering loose like a deadly steel cloth in the savage wind; torn rigging snapping at ship and crew alike; and the occasional spark of red-tinged electricity crackling over it all. Hunter shook his head at the sight.

"Bloody hell," Captain Hunter swore, "it's quite the mess."

"Aye, Captain, it is," Mr. Whitehorse agreed. "Fortunately, it doesn't look so far gone that it might could be patched until we reach port."

As the two men watched, a bolt of lightning struck the errant mesh, illuminating it a moment as the raw electrical power was transferred along the net, recharging the ship's batteries. No sooner had the electricity faded than another rigging line snapped due to the wind. Immediately, one of the three sailors trying to get the net under control turned and raced off across the deck. He returned a moment later with hooked poles.

Armored in rubber gauntlets to protect themselves from the electricity, the three sailors navigated the ruined mesh with a practiced grace - the kind of grace born from years of experience in dangerous storms. Grabbing the lines, the crewmen hauled away at cables attached to the steel mesh frame, which flared out away from the ship like a large pair of wings. This netting caught and channeled the dispersed lightning into barrel-shaped Daniell cell batteries stored below decks.

Two cables towards the bow swung wild in the wind, above crewmen fighting to bring them under control with hooked poles. William ran up and relayed the captain's instructions while Whitehorse and Hunter unsecured the starboard winch and hauled away.

Steadily, the damaged mesh was drawn in, rolled like so much fabric. Once the netting was coiled against the ship's side, Mr. Whitehorse began tying it down with William's assistance. As the five worked feverishly, Captain Hunter stalked across deck towards the bow though the hammering rain, as if oblivious to the storm's futile efforts to wash him over the side.

"Mr. O'Fallon! What's been happening to my ship?" Hunter shouted over the rain.

The man Hunter addressed turned at hearing his name. Wiping rain water from his eyes, the quartermaster reached up to squeeze the rainwater from the long, braided red lock that extended from the sole island of hair on his head.

"Torn cables, Cap'n, storm's too much for them. Been needin' replacement now onto a good month or more. Ah'd been hopin' to be gettin' more once we reach port for Moira or Kylee to be usin' for repairs."

Hunter scowled at the cable ends as if he could frighten them into repairing themselves. Lifting one carefully, the captain lightly touched frayed strands.

"We just put these in two or three months back?" Hunter asked.

"Aye, three tae the day, nearly. But we've been storm chasin' a wee more'n normal," Conrad replied.

"I'd gauge it only a sight more than normal. But I could've lost count in all the cargo runs to and from the mining towns. Besides, look close there at the threads," Hunter said, gesturing with the frayed end of the cable. "They look cut to me, not ripped," he added.

"We be deep in the middle of a blow Cap'n. Cut by what?" the quartermaster said, wiping rain from his eyes. "There nae be but us out here."

"That's what bothers me. Let Moira know we may need her at her forge for a patch," the captain said, handing over over the ruined cable to O'Fallon. "In the meantime, keep your eyes peeled."

"Aye, Cap'n," Conrad replied with a small nod.

"Oh, and what's this I hear about 'red lightning'?" Hunter asked curiously.

"Ah canna say, Cap'n. It struck so fast, Ah can't be sayin' that Ah saw anythin'," The quartermaster replied.

"Indeed," the captain said thoughtfully. "Keep a sharp eye about you, if it was actual red lightning, then that means nothing good."

Suddenly, a gust of wind struck the *Brass Griffin* broadside, scattering crew across the deck. The wood protested in anguish as timbers groaned and rigging threatened to snap while the ship rotated. Ropes holding barrels in place stretched while wet, frayed hemp popped and unwound rapidly. The first of the barrels leaped free of its bindings, and slammed against the main mast. Rigging popped in the wind, slapping the wet canvas of the gas bag overhead.

Immediately, as the ship listed, Captain Hunter and his crew scrambled across the deck, like mountain climbers scaling a wet cliff face. On reaching the far side, they released a set of lines, pulling open small trim sails used specifically to correct the airship when she turned too hard against the wind. Another moan filled the air; a groan from wood and metal echoing like an abused soul just freed from purgatory.

As the ship finally righted after a few minutes' fight, Hunter and O'Fallon spotted two figures laying on the deck: One sported a hurt arm, the other a nasty bruise already forming on his forehead. William Falke raced over to a crewman who was clutching his arm against his chest.

"Someone find Thorias and tell him we've got two comin' down for treatment!" The young man called out.

While the wounded were carried below, Captain Hunter's eyes searched the clouds, scouring them as if seeking a sign. With a glower as dark as the storm that surrounded him, Hunter stalked away into the driving rain towards the bow of he vessel.

O'Fallon glanced at Krumer Whitehorse. "What be the Cap'n on about?"

"The captain does not like this kind of storm. Never does. He lost his hand in such a storm," Krumer explained, wiping rain from his eyes.

"Ah remember the story. Twasn't a storm the way Ah heard it, but some beastie?" O'Fallon asked curiously.

"After a fashion," the first mate replied matter-of-factly, "it was a beast."

A bright flash of lightning lit the sky the same moment an explosion of sound washed over the ship. Again, the *Brass Griffin* pitched, fighting against the wind slapping her across the bow. Crewmen clung to nearby hand holds, belaying pins, rigging, whatever stable surface they could find. Before the ship settled, it lurched once more. A hard groan of timbers followed a pair of sharp pops. Krumer and O'Fallon exchanged a glance.

"Ah'd be knowin' pistol shot, even in this blow. Shot came

from near the bow, Ah be thinkin'," the quartermaster said.

"Precisely," Krumer replied in alarm. "Which is where the Captain is!"

Hunter's voice cut through the howl of wind, "All hands! To arms!"

Chapter 3

Again gunshots echoed through the rain. There at the bow, Captain Hunter stood rooted to the deck, smoking pistols aimed at the monstrous form of a lightning drake which had materialized out of the clouds.

Thirty feet in length, nearly half the length of the *Griffin* herself, the blue-gray scaled behemoth roared in defiance as it turned to sail dangerously close to the flying schooner's gas bag. Claws flexed and tensed, but only brushed the reinforced material, leaving it undamaged. Eyes as black as obsidian scanned the crew with a predatory glare. With a sharp pop, its leathery wings snapped against the wind, flapping to keep the beast steady on its new perch. Hot steam, wrapped in the pungent odor of overcooked fish, coiled from its mouth in ghostly tendrils. Scars lined the beast's neck and side, old wounds from battles won long ago.

Hunter fired twice more, his shots skimming just past the glistening blue gray scales of the beast. Its black-rimmed, red maw opened in a roaring reply, and Hunter dove to safety as a bolt of deep red lightning scarred the deck where he'd stood. Wood exploded in a shower of splinters while fire erupted where the bolt struck the deck. Taking a sharp turn on the high winds, the drake dipped out of view past the stern.

Quickly, the crew scrambled for their weapons. Some appeared with pistols and knives, others with rifles. O'Fallon handed a revolver to Krumer, who nodded his thanks, then checked the cylinder. Satisfied, the first mate raised his voice.

"Watch sharp! It will make another pass."

Wind tossed loose rigging, tugging at the oilcloth slickers of the crew as a nearby lightning from the storm danced between clouds, arcing across the port side netting with a crackle. Still, no sign of the drake appeared. After a moment, Hunter stirred from the bow and eased towards the railing while flexing his grip on the pistols. Krumer walked up beside him. Below them both, the clouds boiled, with blue-white bolts of lightning leaping between cloud banks like mischievous imps. All the while, the ship plunged ahead, cutting through the gray mists of storm clouds like a knife.

"Bad Omen. You'll ruin a good pistol grip that way," Krumer said casually.

Hunter smiled grimly, realizing he was clenching his clockwork hand again. "It'll be back."

"Of that I've no doubt. It's been stung, but not enough to send it away." Krumer's eyes searched the rolling clouds while lighting danced frantically through the sky. "Are you feeling well?"

"I'm fine, just ... remembering." Hunter replied.

"About the one that took your hand?" Krumer asked, giving the captain a quizzical glance.

"Yes." The captain sighed heavily, wiping rain from his eyes. "Hard memory, that."

"Be wary of this one. I would hate for you to gain another bad omen," the first mate warned, while turning his eyes back to the furious clouds surrounding the ship.

Hunter barked a short laugh. "Point taken!"

The two chuckled, then returned to scanning the storm. Beyond the railing, gray clouds coiled and swirled thickly like a gray soup being constantly churned in a bowl. Rain fell in alternating sheets, drenching ship and crew alike. The wind howled and tugged at the rigging, making the rope twist and crackle as it stretched. However, despite the enthusiasm of the weather, nothing else moved in the clouds.

"It should have struck by now." Krumer said warily.

Hunter frowned. "Something's wrong about this, all of this. It's angry, but why I'll be bloody well damned if I know."

Whitehorse pointed towards a massive shape moving in the soupy clouds, "There! I saw a wing! To arms!"

Almost in reply a shadow broke through the clouds, obscuring the deck. In the next moment an ear-splitting roar muffled any peals of thunder. Through the clouds, the drake dove for the deck, tearing through a few lines of rigging as it landed on the coil of steel mesh stowed on the *Griffin's* starboard side.

Hunter backed a few steps away from the beast, being already at point blank range for his sidearms. In a blur, he raised his brace of pistols and fired. His shots were too hasty and the bullets glanced off the drake's tough hide, skidding along the thicker scales layered at the top of its shoulder. Angered, it swiped a large claw at the captain, tossing him up and back across the deck. He came to a sudden, hard stop against the main mast.

"So much for that idea," he muttered while he flipped open the pistols, dumped the spent shells, and reloaded.

Chapter 4

The drake thrashed about, spitting more bolts of red lightning and snapping at the crew as the hot sting of bullets bounced off its scaled hide. When the first volley of gunfire from the crew had subsided, the drake leaned back on its hind legs to swipe with its obsidian-black, razor-sharp foreclaws. Realizing the small annoyances were outside its grasp, the beast sniffed the air experimentally, tensed, then lunged at the largest knot of the scrambling crew -- only to find its left foot tangled in the steel mesh of the starboard lightning net.

Anger turned to surprise, then to panic as the drake realized it was securely caught. Frantically it jerked, tore, and clawed at the mesh, causing the metal and rope holding it in place to pop free of the ship! The drake roared defiantly. With renewed vigor, the it ran a long tongue over its fangs while it stalked forward across the deck, dragging the ruined mesh behind it.

Conrad O'Fallon knelt next to the railing on the port side behind one of the lightning cannons and reloaded his revolver. "What be the beastie after?" the Scotsman asked over the roar of the storm.

Krumer reloaded his sidearm, "If it were food, there is easier prey than a ship. However, this could be its hunting grounds."

"Supposedly they kin be hearin' the buzz o' the lightning in the batteries an' it be aggravatin' them." Conrad replied.

20

"Tall tales," the first mate scoffed, brushing the rain from his face. "If that were true, there would be drake attacks all along the shipping lanes."

"Either way, this beast is a threat to the crew and ship," Hunter declared flatly. "Cannon will get rid of it, but the body would tangle up things worse. Pistol and rifle shot will chase it off or kill it eventually, but it'll make a mess of the rigging by then." He looked at his first mate, "Krumer, get one of those Daniell cell barrels up here."

Krumer gave Hunter a measuring look before he spoke, "Right away, Captain."

"Be havin' a plan, Cap'n?" O'Fallon asked, watching William run off to ferry a box of ammunition to some of the crew near the far side of the vessel.

"That I do. It's a bad one, more'n likely, but I'm all out of good ones."

"Well, at least it'll be interestin'," Conrad said with a smirk.

Moments later, Krumer shoved one of the brass and rubber barrels up through the cargo hatch to Hunter and O'Fallon. The two men rolled the barrel to the deck while Hunter waved a hand toward a storage locker near the quarterdeck's steps.

"O'Fallon, haul out a length of rope from storage. We're going to use this to knock that drake loose and maybe knock some of the fight out of her."

"Aye!"

Hunter turned his eyes back to the drake while it shook its head angrily at another volley of pistol shot. For a moment, a stray thought nagged at him. He frowned, trying to remember what it was, but the sliver of memory eluded him. He wiped a sheen of rainwater from his eyes as Krumer emerged from below.

"Krumer, that vampire we tossed ashore, Broggins. Did anyone get a look at that 'personal' cargo he had?" Hunter asked, glancing across the deck to look for the drake. Towards the bow, the creature lashed out with a massive paw, narrowly missing three of the crew.

"Not I." Krumer replied.

Just then, Conrad raced back across the deck through the driving wind and rain.

"O'Fallon!" Hunter called, "What of you? Get a look at that odd cargo we got fined for supposedly having?"

Conrad looked surprised. "Tha' damn vampire's? Nae so to be recallin' it, but Ah be rememberin' a peculiar symbol stamped on the small crate. Looked mostly smudged but Ah could be makin' it out in part. It looked tae be a bow an' arrow on a compass." The Scotsman shrugged.

Captain Hunter swore viciously. "Wayfinder's Guild. Among all else they do, they study unusual creatures, like lightning drakes."

Krumer and O'Fallon exchanged a confused glance while Hunter shook his head in disgust. Towards the bow, the drake roared again in anger. Wood splintered, shattering as if struck by a fist. Gunfire barked in reply.

"Damn that man, I bet he did," Hunter swore viciously. Krumer and O'Fallon gave the captain a befuddled look. Hunter waved a dismissive hand.

"Well, never mind all that, I'll explain later. Now tie me off. I've got to get that barrel close to that drake," he explained slipping the leather loop over his revolver to secure it into its holster. "Once close, I'll cut the lines that have the mesh fouled to its leg. Krumer, hold fast the rope; and O'Fallon, shoot the barrel at one of its connections once the drake is free and the barrel close by. It'll spark and that'll make the drake spit lightning. That much lightning at once will blow it sky high and hopefully knock the beast free."

O'Fallon looked shaken at the idea, but nodded nonetheless. "Aye, Cap'n."

"I should go." the first mate declared sternly.

"Krumer, we don't have time to argue. I need your strength here keeping this rope secure. Of the three of us, you're the strongest. O'Fallon is the better shot."

The first mate turned that idea over and found he liked it no better than he did the first time. When he could not come up with an alternative, he frowned, and then lashed one end of the rope to the mast and the other end to Captain Hunter.

"Spirits watch over you, then." Krumer said. He gripped the captain by the shoulder with a hard, calloused green hand for a moment, then let it fall away.

Hunter smiled at his old friend. "I hope so; I'll take any help I can get."

The sound of screams and the snapping of wood filled the air. On the far side of the vessel, the drake snapped its stained, ivory sharp teeth at the ship's gunner, a dwarfish man named Flick. The gunner ducked under the massive creature's bite, rolled forward into a crouch, and squeezed the triggers of his twin Colt pistols. The bullets tore past the drake's right eye, making the beast flinch.

Again the drake snapped at the man, narrowly missing by inches; the beast's teeth did not, however, miss the mast, which took a sizeable crack in the wood as payment. Angered at missing the small figure, the drake sidestepped and shook loose rainwater from its hide. The motion rippled along its muscular frame, just intense enough to dislodge the steel mesh from the reptile's leg. Along the entire length of the *Brass Griffin*, the ship shuddered violently.

"It's free! We're out of time!" Hunter shouted over the wind.

Chapter 5

Whitehorse scrambled to finish the knot while Hunter shoved the barrel onto its side.

O'Fallon nodded. "Luck, Cap'n."

"I may need it," Hunter replied, then charged the drake, rolling the barrel rapidly across the deck.

A few yards away, the flying reptile, unaware of the pending danger, snapped its jaws at two of the crew brandishing harpoons. The drake bit down once, then twice at the nimble figures. However, this only earned the beast a sharp rap on the side of the head as one of the crew managed to use his harpoon like a club. With a roar, the reptile jerked its head away from harm, then batted the crewmen with a massive paw. The two men were hurled across the deck like toys.

Anthony was only a few feet away when the beast heard the rumble of the barrel. It sensed danger, and lashed out at the captain. Too close to the drake to change direction, Captain Hunter vanished from sight beneath the its claws.

"Cap'n!" O'Fallon yelled, jerking his rifle up to his shoulder. The quartermaster took quick aim, but hesitated when the Captain reappeared again, flying up off the deck as the drake yanked at the rope attached to Anthony! O'Fallon kept the iron sights of the rifle square on the barrel, but again hesitated.

Anthony crashed into the drake's side. Immediately, the reptile snatched him up in a massive paw. The rope securing Captain Hunter to the mast went rigid, then started to fray. At the other end, Krumer braced his feet against the rough wooden mast; his teeth were bared in a determined snarl, his arms flexing while he strained to prevent the rope from slipping free of the mast.

"O'Fallon! Shoot!" Hunter yelled over the storm. The captain winced as a searing pain burned along his left side and arm when the drake flexed its paw. At the beast's feet, the barrel and its volatile contents lumbered back and forth in time to the rocking motion of the *Brass Griffin*.

"Cap'n, ye'll get caught when she blows!" Conrad yelled back.

"Damn it, man! Fire!" Anthony snapped.

"Shoot, O'Fallon! Now!" Whitehorse added with a roar.

Reflexively, the quartermaster shouldered the rifle and squeezed the trigger. His shot struck home, ricocheting off the large connector of the insulated barrel. Startled, the drake spat a burst of hot red lightning at the barrel, overcharging two Tesla coils and canisters of zinc and copper sulphate.

The blast engulfed the barrel, drowning it in a torrent of primal energy. At first, nothing happened, other than the wooden skin of the container immediately turning a scorched black. The barrel split apart in a blinding explosion, unable to house the wash of power and heat that rapidly built up inside. As flash and sound subsided, both the drake and Captain Anthony Hunter had completely vanished. Where they had been, a hole was gouged out of the deck plates, and the section of railing behind was completely missing. For a moment – the space of two heartbeats – the main deck was deathly calm. All that could be heard was the rain pounding out a rhythmic, almost staccato, sound like the tapping of a telegraph key. The *Griffin* seemed to moan sullenly, as if in pain.

"Check the netting!" Mr. Whitehorse ordered, pointing to the ruined steel mesh that hung loose from the ship's starboard side.

Those not stunned either ran for the rail to reel in the battered mesh or helped those who suffered the direct impact of the blast to regain their senses. Krumer and O'Fallon looked over the railing at the rolling storm clouds, searching for any sign of Captain Hunter or the drake. William quickly scaled the rigging to one of the lookout's stands attached to the gas bag's frame, high above. All around the vessel, the clouds boiled and churned like thick, curdled milk that had been turned a sickly gray. Eyes scanned the storm, but there was no sign of the flying reptile or the captain.

"Damn it all! Krumer, dae ya think there be a chance?" O'Fallon asked quickly.

Krumer closed his eyes for a moment and sighed deeply. "There's always that, however slim it may be. Mr. Wilkerson! Come about! Lay us into that cloudbank, four degrees down!"

A shout returned from the pilot's wheel, "Aye, Sirrah!" With another groan of taxed wood and metal, the *Griffin's* trim sails tilted, and the vessel bow nosed down at an angle. The thick bottom layer of thunderclouds loomed ahead of the ship.

O'Fallon gave the first mate a concerned look. "How long dae we look?"

"We'll look as long as we're able," Krumer replied, a tired sound to his voice. "Spirits willing, we'll find him. Captain Hunter never leaves crew if he can help it, and neither will we."

"If there's anything tae be findin'," Conrad added.

"We'll find him," Krumer said with a heavy sigh, then wiped rain and damp dreadlocks from his face. The orc stared off into the boiling gray sky, his own thoughts mirroring the view. He knew from long association that Anthony Hunter was a rather stubborn man, especially with regards to his potential demise. The first mate recalled when Anthony had faced off against another lightning drake in defense of the *Griffin* and some of her crew. By the time the drake had been driven off, despite all appearances at having been crushed under the animal's claws, Captain Hunter had instead only lost his hand. Something deep inside Krumer whispered to him that this time would be no different. Hunter would find a way.

"Spirits willing," Krumer said again, "we'll find him."

Chapter 6

A sapphire blue sky with the occasional puff of clouds stretched wide over the ramshackle port town of Briggs' Reach. Ships in their coming and goings dotted the small fishing town's harbor and sky. Of anyone, the broad-shouldered Peter Townsend was as recognizable a feature in Briggs' Reach as the brightly colored fishing cottages in the town. A former sky pirate, then later privateer for the Queen, Pete was rarely surprised these days. It was a unique qualification, so he was told, that made him well suited as dockmaster for Briggs' Reach. However, as the *Brass Griffin* touched water and drifted toward an empty slip in the docks, he whistled low in astonishment.

"Ahoy aboard!" Townsend bellowed to the *Griffin*, lighting his pipe and walking toward the damaged schooner. The dockmaster had witnessed ravaged airships before, but this much wreckage a person just did not see every day on a ship still air-worthy

The *Griffin's* bow was scoured with long, clawed gashes. The grooves were cut deep into her timbers, but fortunately stopped above the waterline. Blackened wood, burnt and pitted, marred the remaining railing and belaying pins along the length of her port side. The sails were stained with soot and peppered with small charred holes. Through some miracle the gas bag itself seemed dirty, but intact.

Krumer appeared on the quarterdeck a moment later while two of the crew scrambled to the dock to tie off the mooring lines.

The first mate held up a hand at the dockmaster's call and waved with a tired smile. "Ahoy, Townsend!"

Peter took a slow pull off his pipe, scowling at the *Griffin's* damage, "looks like ya took a beatin' this trip. What took ta chewin' on ya?"

"Lightning drake," Krumer replied with a brittle tone.

Townsend glanced up at Krumer for a moment when he heard the orc's harsh tone. The dockmaster simply nodded in acknowledgement before he continued to survey the damage, "ah, they can make a mess of a ship. I heard tell of one causin' a fair share of trouble along the shipping lanes. Good ta see ya still sailin'. So, Cap'n Hunter about?"

Krumer hesitated, "missing since the drake attack. Beast took him overboard."

Townsend took a thoughtful pull from his pipe, letting a respectful quiet settle between them. Eventually, he replied, "my sympathies, lad; he was a good Captain."

The first mate set his mouth in a thin line, then folded his thick, scarred arms over his chest. He scowled from beneath the black dreadlocks that framed his face, "missing isn't lost, Peter. We've hope, still. We didn't find a body on ground."

Townsend finally tore his attention away from the condition of the *Griffin*. He gave Krumer a sad, understanding look. "Good ta keep hopes up, but at a good sailin' height ... how'd he be able to survive?" The dockmaster blew out a ring of smoke that coiled about his head, "yer likely chasin' phantoms lad. Not that I blame ya. Been chasin' my own, lately. So much so, I've been neglectin' checkin' all the ships comin' in over the past few days."

"Why? Is something wrong?" Mr. Whitehorse replied.

Townsend frowned a moment while he dredged up the recent events in his mind. "Had some odd thefts lately. Little things, like a pair of iron padlocks, one combination lock. A few burlap sacks that happened to have some salted fish. What worries me is the dead rabbit I found just yesterday."

"Missing locks, that is odd. What was so off about the rabbit?" The first mate asked, his curiosity piqued.

"Drained dry," the dockmaster explained, "throat torn out."

A young man, human, dressed in a loose shirt, brown trousers and worn shoes skid to a stop along the boardwalk, calling out in their direction, "Oy! Ya the *Brass Griffin*?"

Krumer gave Pete a look. The dockmaster shrugged and puffed on his pipe. Once the gangplank was tossed down, the first mate walked to the dock proper and raised his voice in return.

"We're the *Griffin*. State your business," Mr. Whitehorse replied.

The young man drug his eyes from the gaping wounds in the ship, then glanced uncertainly between the dockmaster and Krumer. "Ah'm from the *Black Morgan*. We picked up somethin' o' yers less'n a day back."

"Picked up what? What's your name, boy? An where's the *Morgan* tied at?" Krumer asked sternly.

"Name's Johnny and we're at pier twelve. But wha' yer

wantin's at the infirm'ry, backside o' the apoth'cary," Johnny replied, jerking a thumb over his shoulder.

The first mate raised an eyebrow, "indeed? Tell your Captain, the *Griffin* thanks him for the message. Fair winds to you, boy." Krumer fished two pence out of his pocket and tossed to the boy.

"Aye!" The young man raced off down the docks the way he came.

Pete took another draw on his pipe. "Think it's Hunter?"

Krumer sighed, "Spirits willing."

Chapter 7

Krumer navigated through the maze of brightly-colored, squat buildings in the direction indicated by the boy from the *Black Morgan*. Initially, the first mate had no trouble finding his way along the ancient, damp cobblestones while he threaded his way through the town. It was not until he reached a fishmonger's shop painted a cheery blue and aptly named 'The Blue Fishery' that Krumer realized he might actually be lost.

With a brief look overhead at the clear mountain sky, he set his jaw and quickly pressed onward. Krumer stepped around the corner of the fishmonger and set his course for the east side of the fishing town. His determination was rewarded a few minutes later when he saw a weathered sign for BeeBottles' Apothecary. The first mate stepped through the door and inside.

Somewhere above the door, the jingle of bells stopped Krumer up short just inside the doorway. The apothecary was a modest, square building. Wooden shelves easily taller than Krumer's height subdivided the room into narrow sections. On these, all manner of items from rope to pickled herring, and even a few cans of bicarbonate soda were neatly arranged.

An older woman, black hair shot through with streaks of gray all gathered into a proper bun atop her head, shuffled out in a blue gingham dress from behind the farthest shelf. She tilted her nose down to peer at the orc over her square framed glasses.

"And what can I do for you, young man?" she asked, her voice colored with a very faint French accent. "Be a dear and shut the door? We rather not let the stiff breeze in too often."

The first mate shut the door behind him and fidgeted. "I was told you have an infirmary, madam? Also that you may have a patient? A rather determined man?"

A bemused smile spread across her face that seemed to warm the room. "Certainly! And if you are the 'Mr. Whitehorse' he keeps speaking of, your friend will be very pleasantly surprised. Step behind the counter, and take the hall to the back rooms. He will be eager to see you."

Krumer nodded his thanks with a sideways grin, then vanished behind the counter.

A short walk later, the first mate knocked on the door frame of a long room that held a pair of beds. Each bed had its own nightstand and was separated by a cream curtain on a simple frame that ran the same length as the beds. Captain Hunter looked over from the first bed and smiled at his first mate in the doorway. The captain tried to rise, but winced instead and settled back onto the pillow. With a small shake of his head, Krumer walked into the room.

"Well, spirits do favor the foolish and Anthony Hunter. How are you?" Mr. Whitehorse asked with a smile that did not quite conceal his concern,

Hunter chuckled then winced in pain again. "Damnable cracked rib, hurts bloody awful. Aside from that, I'm alive. I don't see me wrestling any more drakes soon, though."

"That would relieve the crew. Mr. O'Fallon, in particular."

When the pain subsided, Hunter sighed. "Krumer, I know what stirred that drake to action. Sad to say, we helped irritate the whole thing."

The first mate pulled up a chair and took a seat next to the bed. "What do you mean?"

"When Broggins was aboard, he mentioned something about a prize. He boasted that it would set him up for quite awhile. I've a firm thought that he meant a drake egg. Skies above, it'll be a hatchling if we're unlucky."

Krumer frowned. "Briggs' Reach isn't as wide as it is tall, but it's still a rat's nest enough when it wants to be. The egg of a lightning drake is valuable to the right buyer, despite how illegal it is to sell or transport an 'animal dangerous to the general populace' like a drake. Why Broggins, though? Not that I'd mind turning him in for it."

"After the explosion, both the drake and I flew clear. As luck had it, I woke first, falling next to her. I quickly wrapped what was left of my rope around the drake's snout before she came to," Hunter explained.

Krumer raised an eyebrow, "well, at least you weren't about to say you rode on the back of flying turtles, I might not believe you. So the drake was a she?"

"Hold to, we're sailing towards that port," Hunter continued, "We struggled against each other a good bit, but that explosion took a lot of fight from her. She flew us back towards her roost and tossed me off on a ledge nearby. While I pondered where I'd landed, I noticed an old campsite. It had been used for observing the drake nests – I've seen those before. I was searching the campsite when the *Black Morgan* found me."

"I see, but how do you know it had anything to do with Broggins?"

"Hand me my coat, would you?" the captain asked.

Krumer handed Hunter his coat and the captain dug a weathered, but intact, brass pocket watch from a breast pocket. On the watch, an inscription of 'A. Hunter' was still clearly visible despite some tarnish and weathering.

"Even though it's a bit battered, I'd know my pocket watch anywhere. There were bits and pieces of Wayfinder Guild gear about, as well. The kind used to capture a drake to tag them for study. Once I convinced the *Morgan* I wasn't there to loot the camp – and that's a bloody lively story for another time – they explained that they run supplies for the scientists when they're out and about. Seems they remembered carrying a crate out from the camp many days back. They took it towards the Brittany coast."

Krumer nodded in understanding, "which is where we picked it up with Broggins almost glued to it. It was carried in the wrong direction and he was trying to get it out here. But why?"

The captain shook his head. "Bloody hell if I know. Once we find Broggins, I plan on asking him straight away. The way I see it, we just need to get that egg out of town, and out to that clutch. Once she sees it, this all should solve itself. "

Krumer nodded and rose. "I've an idea where Broggin's would go, Anthony. There aren't many who'll traffic in drake eggs here."

"Get Townsend to put his pipe down and help you beat the bushes. There's no telling where he might've stashed it. Broggins isn't the smartest man, but he's not entirely a fool. He'll keep it carefully hidden."

      "Understood. Stay and rest. I'll send O'Fallon and Moira along to collect you. I will handle Broggins." With a feral gleam in his eye, Krumer left on his way. Captain Hunter settled into his own thoughts and gazed towards the partially open window through which the dim sounds of a dock, busy with the coming and goings of merchant ships, drifted into the room.

Chapter 8

"Beggin' the Cap'n's pardon?" A voice said, breaking the stillness of the room.

Startled, Hunter opened his eyes. The mid-afternoon sun streamed through the narrow window near the captain's bed. Dust danced in the sunlight. Anthony frowned as he sat up, looking for the source of the voice. The speaker was a smallish man, dressed in worn but clean overalls and a coat. A speckle of gray decorated his hair and a twinkle shone in his blue eyes. He leaned on his broom for support. Captain Hunter nodded for the man to continue.

"Thankee Cap'n. My name's Wilkins," the small man said. "I'm the groundskeeper for the hospice here. Beggin' ye favor but I couldna help but hear ya words with the big bloke a moment ago. Ye lookin' for a drake egg, are ya?"

Cautious of his ribs, Hunter sat up slowly in bed, eyeing the man suspiciously. "Yes, I did say that. Why do you ask?"

"I might be someone who knows a bit about it," the groundskeeper explained. "Yer first mate will be tearin' up the waterfront, but he'll not find a thing. The drake egg yer lookin' for sits in a warehouse near the old dockmaster's office where the old North docks used to be."

The captain considered that a moment. "Mind you, I'm grateful for any words of help you might have but, naturally, I am suspicious. Drake eggs are valuable. In some places men would kill to have one of the blasted things."

Wilkins chuckled and continued to lean on his broom. "What's in it fer me ya might say? Good question Cap'n, and a sound one to be sure. I've my own business with the man ye named a bit ago."

"Broggins?" Anthony asked.

"Aye, that's the one. Cap'n, have ya stopped ta wonder where that dandy of a vampire got his funds ta even try most a' his venture? Sure he stole from ya, but a body cannae steal all the way to a drake's nest and back. That's where the rub lies, ya see. Cheated me out of a good portion of ma savings in a game of poker, he did." Wilkins explained. "I think he used some of that vampire mesmerism! Now, I'm not a man who owns much, nor oft do I care to, but what I do have I'd like ta keep and enjoy. The way I see it here? It's only right that Broggins lose what he stole my money in the first place ta get."

"If you have a grudge and know where it is, why not turn him in, yourself?" Hunter asked.

Wilkins chuckled again, "well Cap'n, my word isn't as good as it used ta be in many circles. Townsend would take some convincin' and then there's makin' it stick."

Hunter eased himself from his bed and reached for his coat. He was suspicious of the man's story, but if any of it was true, that meant the drake's egg was within his reach. It was a chance he would have to take. At worst he would look foolish, something he had suffered before in his life and expected to probably suffer again in the future. Once he was fully dressed, the captain walked to the doorway and paused to look over his shoulder.

Captain Hunter frowned, "how can you be so sure it's there?"

"Fair enough question," the groundskeeper replied with a shrug. "I like takin' a constitutional along the old North docks in the evenin'. The air comin' in is cool, ya see, and helps ease me inta the evenin'. Well a night or so back, I'm walkin' along and what am I seein'? Why the very man who cheated me outta my money!" Wilkins shrugged, "well, naturally, I followed him thinkin' ta turn him inta Dockmaster Townsend. He lost me near the warehouses up there, but I saw he twas' carryin' a bag of meats and such. More'n his like would need. Now hearin' yer tale, that bag makes sense ta me. He had ta been stockin' up ta feed the beast when it hatched from it's shell."

"My thanks, Wilkins. I'll see that any money I recover comes back to you," Anthony replied with a smile.

A twinkle of mischief shone in Wilkins' eye. "Kind of ye Cap'n, but nae necessary. I'll know when ye've got the egg and Broggins be in the Dockmaster's tender care. At times like these, the Reach does become quite a small little place." Wilkins winked, "besides, a good drake shell's worth it's own bit o' money."

With a faint smile, Hunter nodded, "true enough. Luck, then."

"Good trackin', Cap'n," Wilkins' replied.

Anthony turned away, and with a fast walk marred by a slight limp, hurried out of his room. Quickly, he traversed the short wooden hallway that connected the apothecary from the infirmary proper. At the entrance to the apothecary, an older woman with black hair shot with streaks of gray held out a hand, and gave Anthony a stern look.

"Where do you think you're goin'?" She asked.

Hunter shook his head, "All due respect, Mrs. BeeBottles, to stop a bungler who has aspirations of being a very bad man."

The proprietor's wife folded her arms across her chest, doing her best to block the doorway. "You need to be in that bed, restin' after what you've been through!"

Suddenly, Hunter gripped the woman by the shoulders. He winced, and moved her gently aside, ignoring her wordless exclamation of shock. The captain shook his head while he quickly limped past. "Madam, I only wish I could, but right now is not the time for this! I'll rest later, you have my word!"

Once past Mrs. BeeBottles, he hurried through the shop then out the front where he stumbled into O'Fallon, who had just opened the door. O'Fallon stepped back in surprise, almost jostling into Moira, the *Brass Griffin*'s blacksmith, her brownish-red hair pulled back in a neat braid. The pair exchanged a glance as Captain Hunter caught himself against the doorframe and sighed, ignoring the sore stiffness that permeated his ribs and leg.

O'Fallon gave Hunter a surprised look. "Cap'n? What're ye doin'? We came tae help ye over tae the *Griffin*."

"If at all," Moira added with a narrow look at Captain Hunter's slightly pale complexion. She reached for his arm, "we should be takin' ya right to a bed, too. Ya look a few paces from death's door. Here, lean on me while we go, Cap'n."

Hunter waved away the man's concern and Moira's offer to support him on his wounded side. "I'm appreciative, but there's a last bit of business we need to see to."

"That'd be?" O'Fallon asked curiously.

"Catch an egg thief or at least his ill-gotten egg," Hunter replied. "I'll explain on the way."

Chapter 9

The North docks, the original docks of Briggs Reach that had been ruined by a storm fifteen years before, sat draped in the late afternoon shadows. All that remained of the dock was a jumble of weathered and broken wooden pylons that thrust up out of the brown harbor water. The few original buildings, like warehouses and the old dockmaster's office, remained firmly intact despite the assault of weather and time. Outside the warehouses, Captain Hunter limped forward, followed by O'Fallon and Moira.

"This be the place, Cap'n?" O'Fallon asked, glancing around.

Anthony frowned while he, too, looked around. He finally replied, "yes, I believe so."

O'Fallon nodded and gave the dilapidated building a measured look. Moira shook her head slightly. "Can we put trust in that Wilkins?"

"If we want to bring this to a close, Moira, this is as good a chance as any. O'Fallon, take the right side, Moira, the left. I'll strike in through here. Shout if you come across anything."

"Cap'n? Ye'll be needin' this." O'Fallon pulled a spare pistol from his belt and handed to Hunter.

The captain accepted the weapon. "True enough, I have felt a bit underdressed since I lost mine overboard. I'm sure they're stuck in a tree by now somewhere." He looked the pistol over carefully. It was an 1875 Remington Revolver, and well cared-for. He preferred his Schofield, but right now he had little room to complain. Captain Hunter gave them each a glance. "Good hunting to you both."

Once the pair had hurried off, Hunter tightened his grip on the pistol and walked toward the warehouse entrance. The double wooden doors were closed, but the opened lock hung loose on the door hasp just below the latch. Hunter paused to listen. He could hear muffled sounds that seemed to emerge from deep inside the warehouse.

Satisfied the door was safe enough, he eased it open and slipped inside. The interior of the warehouse was in no better shape than the exterior. Stout beams still withstood the weight of a roof now dilapidated and weathered with age. A few dusty crates remained, old shipments long forgotten by their owners. Hunter walked slowly around these and navigated the main warehouse in the dim light. Twice he heard birds stir overhead when they were startled by a noise from somewhere inside the building. Slowly, he moved farther into the building.

Once Anthony had come abreast of a cluster of rotten crates, the sound of wood sliding against weathered wood – like that of a window being opened slowly in hopes of not drawing any attention – caught his ears. The captain hesitated, crouching low against the crates, pistol at the ready. Birds stirred again in the rafters, and then he heard voices in whispered conversation. Hunter relaxed slightly; he guessed it was either O'Fallon or Moira taking advantage of a window in poor state of repair. The captain stepped beyond the crates upon hearing a faint, guttural snarl, followed by an odd scratching sound in the distance. He stopped and strained his ears. After a moment, he heard the sound again. Then a moment later, yet again. Setting his bearing on what he thought was the source, he eased deeper among the dusty shafts of light.

It was a few minutes more before the source of the sound appeared. There, in the back of the building sat the squat, winged figure of a small drake, only a foot or so taller than a large dog. It was a hatchling. Given its size it could not have been more than a few days old. The drake was intent on something above it. Every few minutes it would take a deep breath, gather its strength, and with all the clumsy grace of a youngling, leap up with a mad flutter of immature wings. At the peak of its jump, it would snap at a wiggling object that hung from a rafter. The object – a thin, pale man dressed in workman denim with a threadbare coat – swung like a worm on the end of a fishing line, his eyes wide with frustration and panic. Hunter stepped forward carefully to not startle the hatchling. He smiled thinly at the figure on the rafter.

"Bit of trouble, Broggins?" the captain asked, amused.

The thief looked up at his name, nearly losing his precarious position on the beam. "Hunter! Quick! Shoot the bloody thing. It's trying to kill me!"

Hunter glanced at the drake. The reptile, having noticed the newcomer, stopped its eager attempts to grab the danging vampire and stared at the captain. A few light scars could be seen along the little drake's scaled hide as if it had been whipped. The captain looked around, noticing the broken egg shells, bent locks, pieces of canvas that looked passably like banking money bags, and a horsewhip that had been bitten in two. He also noticed a bag on a hook that looked a much more recent addition than the rest of the warehouse items. He recognized the faint smell of freshly cooked salted pork from it.

"I suspect it has plenty reason to. Besides, unless it's learned to use a wooden stake, I fear your vampiric nature will keep you quite whole, though I still suspect the pain of the bites will sting some, even for you." Hunter nodded towards the hatchling. "Trying to train it were you?"

Broggins shifted uncomfortably. "Not in the least! That'd be against the law!"

"So far I've seen nothing that tells me you give a whit for the Queen's law." Hunter slowly eased over, opened the bag, and withdrew a wrapped section of salted pork. "And if you didn't have a goal to train it, why would a vampire need any salted pork? Your game's done. The bent locks and money bags tell enough in my mind that you'd hoped for a pet to use in some robbery."

"Lot that you know, ya blowhard!" Broggins snapped while he adjusted his grip on the rafter.

Sounds of running preceded the arrival of Moira and O'Fallon. Both cast a surprised look at the drake and then Broggins. Hunter tore off small pieces of the pork and tossed it over. After an experimental sniffing, the beast worked slowly at the meat. Hunter showed the rest to Moira.

"Moira, would you be so kind as to find something to soften this for the small one over there. I doubt it has enough teeth yet to do more than gnaw at it."

Moira gave the captain a wide grin, "Aye Cap'n, a bit o' water and a touch o' milk'll do this little baby quite nice. Leave it ta me. I worked for a crew hired by the Royal Geographic Society who had ta take care of a clutch once. They had this idea of markin' then trackin' where they go."

O'Fallon gestured to Broggins, who had not yet left the safety of his rafter but obviously was considering the option. "An' him, Cap'n?"

"Fetch Townsend. Tell him we've found our thieving rascal and he's in dire need of a nice pair of leg irons. That is, until the Queen's men hold their monthly court here. Then he gets to be their problem." Hunter smiled a bit then. "And send word to the *Griffin*. I think it's past time we got this hatchling home."

Epilogue

Branches swayed slightly from a chill wind along the sunlit tree line that decorated the rocky slope. Where the slope left the trees, it ran for several yards before it became a cliff face, rushing downward to the green carpet of the Ardennes in the valley below. A game trail that followed the slope ran between the trees and spilled out onto the cliff face. Beyond the cliff and forest below, the green of the trees spread out like a wool blanket across Glen Coe in the Scottish Highlands. Out of the game trail walked Moira, carrying a bag of dried beef. Not far behind, the three foot tall hatchling scampered nearby. Occasionally the youngling would become distracted by a butterfly, a bird or even the dance of sunlight on its own blue-gray scales, and fall behind. A moment later, it would realize it was alone and run to catch up.

Moira stepped into the clearing at the top of the cliff and pulled open the bag. The beef inside was enough for what she needed. She felt a nudge at her elbow, then heard a plaintive bleat from the young drake. Almond-shaped obsidian eyes passed a sad look between Moira and the bag of dried beef. Moira tried to remain stubborn, but the hatchling drake was persistent. Eventually pleading eyes won over resolve.

"Oh bloody hell. One mind ya, just one now." Moira in a mock-exasperated tone.

The drake squeaked an immature roar in reply, then sat back with its maw of stubby curved teeth wide for the slab of dried beef.

Moira selected a modest-sized section and tossed it over. The drake chewed contentedly.

"Careful Moira, we've only so much." Captain Hunter said, walking slowly up the rocky ground. He leaned heavily on his cane, his broken bones not quite mended from his ordeal. Krumer Whitehorse followed further behind.

Moira smiled, "aye, Cap'n. There's plenty. We can spare a piece or two."

"All right then. Let's lead him over and hope someone's about." Hunter said, looking up at the skies.

"Aye, Cap'n," Moira replied.

Moira withdrew more meat and led the young hatchling, already hungry at the sight of another chance at food, across grass and bald rocks towards the edge of the ridge line. Once there, she tossed the meat to the hatchling and set down the bag. Slowly, she backed away while the hatchling's attention was diverted towards its meal.

Krumer joined both Moira and Hunter closer to the cliff's magnificent view. "Any sign?"

"None yet. However, it's early to tell. She may have moved on."

The first mate shook his head slowly. "Perhaps, perhaps not. Drakes are very territorial and rarely give up a good, safe nest, from what I understand."

The pair scanned the sky before Krumer broke the silence. "Any word over Broggins? You spent quite the time with those barristers."

"Quite. Though, I was glad to be on this particular end of a barrister for a change." Hunter sighed a little and continued. "Broggins had more against him than just planning to pilfer a bank. Four outstanding counts of theft, two of extortion and at least one murder. Though the murder was conjecture."

"No body?" Krumer asked.

The captain shrugged, "indeed. It was suggested it was his own sire. A Lady Vanessa Bellgrave or some such."

Krumer chuckled ruefully. "A backstabbing, evil man no doubt, but he is a clever one."

"You sound as if you admire the man?" Hunter asked slightly surprised.

The first mate shot the captain a sour look. "He's a toad, and a blood sucking one. I'm merely impressed at his ability to survive this long."

Hunter chuckled. "His neck isn't stretched yet, not that it would do much for one of his kind. In either case, the trial was not lengthy. He was much the picture of a braggart, and denied everything with a glib lie for the most of it. When evidence, albeit as thin as ice in spring, was presented of the murder, he grew agitated and practically flew into a rage. Acted as if he never knew. It took five stout lads to hold him down so he could be chained to his chair with blessed manacles. The verdict was quick to return. They'd hang him for sure, but everyone knows that'll do no good. Word is that he'll spend his long days beneath Millbank prison until they decide what to do with him."

"Not a stake through the heart? It would be more effective, waste less time," Krumer said with a derisive snort.

"Ah, there's the rub of it. His crimes merit a hanging - by law there's no provision for a stake through the heart." Hunter paused a moment to recall a memory. "The oddest part I cannot deduce, was why Wilkins was there."

Krumer looked confuse. "The little man from the hospice?"

"The very same," Anthony replied. "I wasn't permitted to hear his testimony. No one was, save the barristers of course. Odd all that secrecy given his story was of a 'gambling debt'. No way of knowing what was said, though."

"Spirits move in their own time and way, Anthony," Krumer explained. "Shamans of my tribe taught that they can be anywhere, when we might need them most, of course."

Hunter considered that a moment, "Quite. I just had not expected one to be cleaning a hospice floor."

An ear rattling roar broke the conversation. From above, an adult drake - the very one that had attacked the *Brass Griffin* - soared overhead, wheeled, then flew close enough that Moira, Hunter and Krumer all were possessed of an instinctive urge to duck. The lightning drake extended her wings and dropped with an unusual grace to the rocky ground. Large, dark reptile eyes shifted uneasily across the three *Griffin* crew. Beside them, the young hatchling sniffed the air curiously while it chewed steadily on the dried beef.

Moira shifted her weight nervously while she watched the adult drake from mere yards away. "Cap'n?"

"Do nothing sudden." He ordered.

"Aye ta that," Moira replied.

Krumer frowned. "It's not often one can be this close to a drake, without losing parts of their body, or more commonly their lives. Present company excluded of course."

Hunter did not reply. His eyes were locked on those of the adult drake. Slowly he took a step forward.

Moira started, but Krumer waved her to be still.

Hunter shook his head and spoke quietly to Moira and Krumer. "Just hold your course. We'll see this through. Moira, toss me some of that beef."

Moira dug out another piece which immediately drew both the attention of the hatchling and adult drake. The hatchling looked from hunger while the adult drake visibly tensed in concern. Moira tossed the dried beef slab to Hunter, who caught it clumsily, thanks to his cane and cracked bones. Quickly, the younger drake hurried over to Hunter and sat nearby, looking between Hunter and the dried beef in earnest.

Hunter looked from the hatching to its mother, "my thanks." He turned his attention to the little drake. "Time for you to be off, little one." With a grunt, Hunter tossed the beef towards the adult drake.

It sailed through the air, but before it could reach the ground, the older drake caught it in a massive paw. Chasing the meat, the younger drake paid little heed to its direction; that is, until it noticed how close it was to the larger drake. The hatchling skidded to an abrupt stop. While it turned its gaze up at its mother, the young drake's eyes glinted with fear and confusion. Slowly, cautiously, the mother dropped the beef to the hatchling and trumpeted. The sound was not as loud as a roar, but actually a deeper, softer song. Surprising since it was made by a several ton reptile. Tentatively, the hatchling took the beef, chewed some of it, then bleated in reply.

"Cap'n, am I seein' this? I never seen a drake act like that before," Moira said incredulously.

Hunter smiled, his own suspicions completely laid to rest.

"Quite right. I'm sure you haven't. Neither have I."

"Animals often do many odd things," Krumer commented, although he sounded less than convinced at his own statement.

Once the young beast was done with the meal of beef, the adult drake nudged the hatchling away from the crew and towards the edge of the overlook. She looked down at her offspring then spread her wings and trumpeted a short burst of notes. The hatchling clumsily mimicked its mother, a passing attempt at best. Suddenly the mother crouched and leaped into the air and off the cliff. The younger drake started forward a few steps, then paused to look back at Moira, Krumer, and Hunter.

Hunter leaned on his cane and smiled. "Go on, now. Your mother is waiting."

The hatchling did not make a sound, but watched the captain for a long moment. It turned toward the edge with a deep breath, then leapt into the air. At first the youngling fell like a rock, but wind caught under immature wings and let the young drake glide for a brief pace. When he lost the wind, his mother caught him deftly and placed him on her back.

"I've heard said that dolphins in the sea are animals," Hunter commented aloud. "Though I've seen those same animals stop to help a sailor for no reason other than the sailor is endangered by, say, a shark. Might as one would help another person just because they are in need. Funny, that."

Beyond the three of them, the adult drake circled in a wide path and looked back at Hunter, her offspring clutching her back and bleating aloud merrily.

Captain Hunter nodded slightly with a ghost of a smile. The

drake returned the nod, banked to the right and flew toward the mountains with a trumpeting roar.

About the Author

C. B. Ash holds degrees as a Physical Scientist and Computer Scientist. Since college, he has run his own networking business, worked as laboratory technician, taught martial arts, and traveled for several years as a software engineering consultant. Currently he shares his time between software architecture, web design and slaving away over outlines for new manuscripts … when he's not keeping his cat off his keyboard.

During that time he has written several fantasy and science fiction short stories, a fantasy/murder mystery novel and several poems. One of which garnered him the Emily Dickinson Award in Poetry. His first novel, *Kinloch*, was published in May, 2004. *Tales of the Brass Griffin: Red Lightning* is one of the *Tales of the Brass Griffin* series. To find out more, visit: http://BrassGriffin.com.

www.ingramcontent.com/pod-product-compliance
Lightning Source LLC
Chambersburg PA
CBHW050912120626
46552CB00004B/1545